MARVEL

EARTH'S MIGHTIEST HEROES!

the AVENGERS

THOR
THE MIGHTY

ADAPTED BY
Elizabeth Rudnick

STORY BY
Christopher Yost & Joshua Fine

WRITTEN BY
Brandon Auman

EXECUTIVE PRODUCER
Alan Fine, Eric S. Rollman, Dan Buckley, Simon Phillips

DIRECTED BY
Vinton Heuck

MARVEL

NEW YORK

Copyright © 2011 Marvel Entertainment, LLC and its subsidiaries. Marvel, The Avengers and all related characters:
TM & © 2011 Marvel Entertainment, LLC and its subsidiaries. Animated Series: © 2011 Marvel Entertainment, LLC and its subsidiaries.
Licensed by Marvel Characters B.V. www.marvel.com. All rights reserved.

Published by Marvel Press, an imprint of Disney Publishing Worldwide. No part of this book may be reproduced or transmitted in any form
or by any means, electronic or mechanical, including photocopying, recording, or by any information storage and retrieval system, without
written permission from the publisher. For information address
Marvel Press, 114 Fifth Avenue, New York, New York 10011-5690.

Printed in the United States of America

First Edition
1 3 5 7 9 10 8 6 4 2
J689-1817-11046

ISBN 978-1-4231-4295-9

www.marvel.com

Inside their ambulance, nurse Jane Foster and her partner heard a "code blue" come over the radio.

Jane raced toward the waterfront. She knew what the code meant: **Super Villains.**

Jane was right! Four Super Villains were attacking the docks! It was the Wrecking Crew! When she jumped out of the ambulance, the villains aimed their weapons at her!

Just as the Super Villan Thunderball was about to fire, he was sent flying through the air! **He had been hit by a giant hammer!**

THOR THE MIGHTY
HAD ARRIVED!

One by one, Thor swatted away the villains—first, he took on Bulldozer, then Piledriver. . .

Finally, only Wrecker was left. He pointed his super powered crowbar at Thor! Their weapons clashed!

Thunderball saw Wrecker under attack. He noticed a large metal crate hanging above Thor. **CRASH!** He knocked it down—right on top of the hero!

But Thor was strong! He smashed his way through the crate. The villains couldn't believe it!

Thor was about to finish them off—but then Wrecker captured Jane!

Wrecker had Thor right where he wanted him! Or so he thought.

Wrecker heard a noise coming from behind him. Turning, he saw Thor's mighty hammer, Mjolnir, flying right at him. **CLANK! Down went Wrecker!**

Thor turned to Jane. "You risked your life to help the wounded," he said. "Why?"

"Because they needed my help," Jane answered.

Just then, a great flash of lightning appeared in the sky. Through it, Thor could see Heimdall, the guardian of the bridge to Thor's world.

"I bear a grim message," Heimdall told Thor. "Asgard is under siege!"

Back in the realm of Asgard, a chill had set in. Frost Giants threw large boulders at the walls of Odin's palace, knocking them down.

Through the icy mist, a figure emerged. **This was Loki, Thor's brother.**

He wanted to rule Asgard!

Thor arrived in Asgard and made his way to the action. He joined his warrior friends. Together, they took out as many Frost Giants as they could.

From his throne in the heart of Asgard, King Odin saw all that happened. He was glad his eldest son had returned. **But he was also worried.**

The ferocious battle continued. The Frost Giants knocked Thor to the ground. He got up, but they kept attacking!

It seemed as if the Mighty Thor had met his match.

A Frost Giant reached out and picked up Thor. Using his hammer, Thor broke the giant's teeth.

"I have felt your wrath, Frost Giants," Thor said. **"Now you shall feel MINE!"**

Summoning all his strength, Thor raised his hammer and called upon its great power. White-hot lightning surged through it, drawing power from Asgard. Then with a loud **BOOM!** it shot through the Frost Giants, destroying them all.

Using his own powers, Loki shot a blast of purple energy at Thor.

"I do not wish to fight you, Loki!" Thor said.

But Loki wanted to fight.

The brothers fought fiercely. Thor with his hammer, Loki with his spear. CLASH! The sound of metal and stone rang out over Asgard. Finally Thor was victorious.

It was time for Loki to face his father, King Odin.

"You have gone too far, Loki!" Odin said. "You leave me no choice. You are hereby banished to the Isle of Silence."

Then he opened the portal to that world and sent his son through.

While his father wanted Thor to stay and help
him on Asgard, the Thunderer knew it was time
to return to Earth.

For now, Asgard was safe. But Loki was not destroyed, only banished to a wasteland. **And he had a plan.**

"No one is ready for what comes next," Loki hissed. He would seek revenge on Thor . . . and Asgard.